Sid the Kid and the Dryer

a story about Sidney Crosby

Story by **LESLEY CHOYCE**   Art by **BRENDA JONES**

NIMBUS
PUBLISHING LTD.
—— NIMBUS.CA ——

Nimbus Publishing Limited
3660 Strawberry Hill Street, Halifax, NS, B3K 5A9
(902) 455-4286 nimbus.ca

Printed and bound in Canada
NB1408
Design: Heather Bryan
Editor: Penelope Jackson

The story idea for this book was originally suggested to the author by John MacIntyre and was greatly appreciated.

Library and Archives Canada Cataloguing in Publication

Title: Sid the Kid and the dryer : a story about Sidney Crosby / story by Lesley Choyce ; art by Brenda Jones.
Names: Choyce, Lesley, 1951- author. | Jones, Brenda, 1953- illustrator.
Identifiers: Canadiana (print) 20190165014 |
Canadiana (ebook) 20190165022 |ISBN 9781771087759 (hardcover) |
ISBN 9781771087766 (HTML)
Subjects: LCSH: Crosby, Sidney, 1987-—Childhood and youth—Juvenile fiction.
Classification: LCC PS8555.H668 S54 2019 | DDC jC813/.54—dc23

Nimbus Publishing acknowledges the financial support for its publishing activities from the Government of Canada, the Canada Council for the Arts, and from the Province of Nova Scotia. We are pleased to work in partnership with the Province of Nova Scotia to develop and promote our creative industries for the benefit of all Nova Scotians.

For Aidan
    – L. C.

I'm probably the most famous clothes dryer in the world. My name's W. P., short for Whirlpool. People come to this museum from all over to look at me. I guess you could say I'm retired. But once upon a time in a basement in Cole Harbour, Nova Scotia, Canada....

Up until we arrived at the Crosby home, I was just an
ordinary dryer. My friend Milton was just an ordinary washer.
We were still shiny and new.

Then two delivery guys drove us from the store in a truck,
carried us down into a basement, and hooked us up.

"*Finally*, we get to see some action," Milton said.

We had the basement to ourselves except for a couple of tall skinny guys named Jack.

"Hi," I said. "What do you two do down here?"

Jack One said, "We've got a pretty important job. We're holding up the house."

Jack Two just nodded.

"Pretty quiet down here," Milton said.

"Just wait," Jack One said.

Soon, a nice woman came downstairs with a load of laundry.

"Oh boy," Milton said. "Finally, we get to show our stuff."
He sloshed and spun away, singing the whole time.

Then it was my turn. The heat felt good and the rolling and
tumbling was my kind of music. Man, this was the life I had

Then it got quiet. Milton thought it was too quiet.

"How're you guys holding up?" he shouted to Jack One and Jack Two.

They laughed. Jack One said, "Man, that's an old one."

"Is it always this quiet?" I asked.

"Just wait," Jack Two said.

So I waited.

I was dozing off when I heard the door slam up above. I heard somebody running.

"Who's that?" I wondered.

Jack One said, "That's the kid. Now things get interesting."

"The kid?" I asked.

"THE kid," he repeated.

And then it happened.

The door above us swung open. I saw feet on the steps. They flew down, hardly touching the stairs. The kid. Ten years old, I think. He had a spark.

The kid ran across the floor, giving a high-five to Jack One and Jack Two. He grabbed a hockey net from a dark corner and came running straight at me. He stopped and gave Milton and me a funny look.

"Welcome to home ice," he said.

He set up the net right alongside me and put on a pair of Rollerblades. He rolled down to the dark corner of the basement. When he came charging back, he was holding a hockey stick and scooting a puck in front of him.

The kid was moving like lightning. When he pulled the hockey stick back, I held my breath.

I heard the smack first and then saw the speeding puck.

I watched as it slammed into the net.

"The name's Crosby, folks; Sidney Crosby!" he shouted. "He shoots! He scores!" The kid looked right at me, winked, and added, "You ain't seen nothing yet."

The kid kept shooting over and over and over. He did figure eights around Jack One and Jack Two until the woman yelled down, "Sidney! Time for supper." He dropped his hockey stick and ran upstairs, the Rollerblades still on his feet.

Then the light went out and it got quiet again.

The next afternoon, the kid came down the stairs again, his feet hammering on every step. It looked like he'd had a bad day.

The first puck that missed the net and hit me below my door knocked the wind out of me.

"Oops," Sidney said, looking at my dent. "Sorry, dude."

The door from upstairs opened. Sidney's mom shouted down, "What was that?"

Sidney gulped. "Nothing."

"You didn't hit my new washer, did you?"

"No," he answered truthfully.

"Well you must have hit something. Be careful!"

"Yes, Mom," Sidney said as he leaned over and studied the bruise in my white enamel.

"It's okay," I told him. "Nobody's perfect."

He seemed a little freaked out that a dryer had spoken to him.

"I've been hit plenty of times," Jack One said. "These things happen. The kid's gotta practice."

"Practice is everything," Jack Two added.

Sidney nodded.

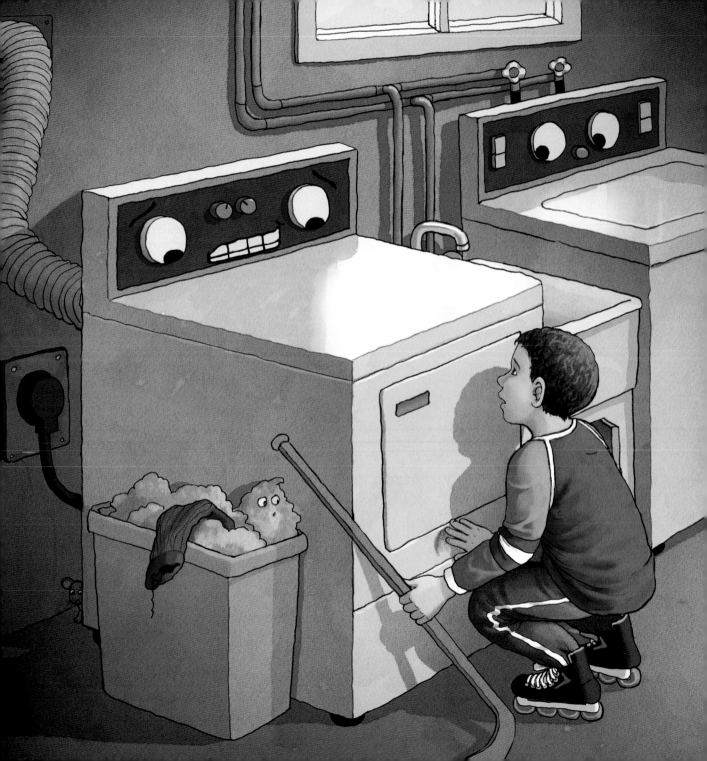

I figured Milton and I had it pretty good in the basement. Sure, we liked our jobs, but the most fun was when Sidney came home. He still missed the net and hit me once in a while. Whenever his mother heard the clang of the puck on my metal she'd stomp the floor above, reminding Sidney to cut it out. Soon I was even missing a knob and one of my buttons. But I could still dry the clothes just fine.

One Sunday afternoon, Sidney had a bunch of older kids over. One of them was really good and shot goal after goal. And he wouldn't let Sidney score a single shot.

After they left, Sidney looked really discouraged. He sat down on the floor in front of me. "I'll never be that good," he said. "What's the point of all this practice?"

He just sat there staring at all the dents he'd put in me. Milton was still shiny and new-looking, but I looked like a piece of old junk.

"Don't worry about it, kid," Jack One said. "It's only a game."

"Yeah, it's only hockey," Jack Two said.

"Keep at it," I said, "and I bet you'll be even better than the big kids."

"But there will always be somebody better than me."

"So what?" I said. "If you're gonna be good at anything, you have to make mistakes along the way. A lot of mistakes."

"Why?"

I couldn't explain it. Anyway, what did I know? I was a dryer, not a sports expert. All I had ever done was get loaded up with wet clothes after Milton did the hard part. Spin them around and turn up the heat. I didn't have dreams of greatness like the kid here. But I had to say something.

"Wouldn't it be amazing," I asked him, "getting up every day and playing, doing something you love?"

But Sidney seemed to have lost that spark I'd seen in his eyes. He still came downstairs after school some days and put on his Rollerblades. He took a few shots, hit the net a few times, then missed and hit me. More than once. He had a faraway look in his eyes. And no high-five for the Jacks, no shouting, "He shoots! He scores!"

The kid was growing up. We were losing him.

One day, Sidney's father came into the basement. I didn't understand what he was up to at first. He took a look at Milton, checked his wires and his hoses, and nodded.

But then he started to study me. He saw my missing knobs, the way my door looked uneven, the many dents where the raw metal was showing behind my white enamel. He looked unhappy as he shook his head.

And then it happened. Sidney's father started to unhook my vent pipe. Then he unplugged me. Milton gave me a look of despair. The two Jacks looked on in horror. What was going on?

I was about to be traded in. Or worse yet, set out at the curb with the trash.

"Do something," I begged Milton.

But there was nothing to be done. As the cord was unplugged, I felt the life start to drain out of me.

And then I heard the front door open upstairs, the familiar
sound of the kid's running shoes on the floor above and then his
footsteps on the basement stairs. He stopped halfway down and
just stood there, staring at his father.

"What are you doing?" he asked.

"Time to get a new dryer," his father said. "Maybe I better
put the new one farther away from the net, eh?"

Then Sidney ran the rest of the way down the steps.
"No way!" he shouted at his father. "We can't!"

"Why not?" his father asked, looking puzzled.

Sidney bent down and studied all the places
I'd been hit by his puck, all
the shots that hadn't made
it into the net.

At first it seemed like he didn't know what to say. Then he picked up my cord and just held it in his hand. "I think I need to remember that my mistakes are okay," he said. "Every time you miss, you're reminded to keep at it and get better."

"You think keeping this old dryer will make you a better hockey player?" Sidney's dad looked really puzzled now.

"I know it will," the kid said. "It will make me the best."

His father smiled and took my cord out of his son's hand. He plugged me back into the wall socket. Then he ruffled the kid's hair and tapped lightly on me. "Time to practice," he said to Sidney. "Time to get back into the game." And he walked back upstairs and closed the door.

"Maybe," Sidney said to me, "I should ask him to have you moved to the other side of the basement."

"No way, kid," I said, smiling. "I want to be right here where the action is."

Jack One added, "That's right, kid. W. P. can take it."

Milton looked at me and said, "That was a close one. We're a team, right? I wouldn't know what to do without you."

"Don't worry," the kid said as he began to put on his Rollerblades. "He isn't going anywhere."

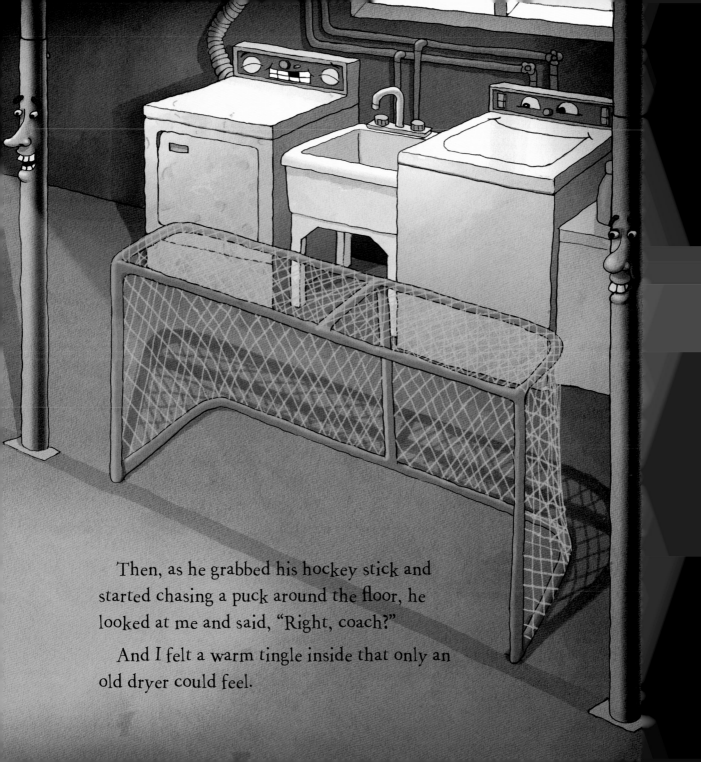

Then, as he grabbed his hockey stick and started chasing a puck around the floor, he looked at me and said, "Right, coach?"

And I felt a warm tingle inside that only an old dryer could feel.

We watched Sidney swoop like a dancer around the basement with his stick and the puck.

He scored goal after goal until he got so dizzy that he made a bad shot. I saw the puck coming my way and braced for impact.

When it made a loud *CARRONG* just above my door,
I heard the familiar stomping of Sidney's mom above.
At that moment, I realized that all would be well here in
the Crosby home in Cole Harbour, Nova Scotia, Canada.
The kid knew that mistakes were okay.

And I knew this kid was on the road to GREATNESS.

About Sidney Crosby

Sidney Crosby (nicknamed "Sid the Kid" because he was only eighteen when he was drafted first overall into the NHL) grew up in Cole Harbour, Nova Scotia. He learned to skate when he was just three years old. As he grew older, Sidney practiced skating and shooting relentlessly, especially in his basement with the now-famous clothes dryer.

He was a star player in minor and junior hockey, which led Sidney to a career with the Pittsburgh Penguins, where he became the youngest person ever to be named captain of an NHL team. He is a legendary hockey player; he has shattered points records, won three Stanley Cups, and helped Team Canada win gold at the 2010 and 2014 Olympic Games. Despite his superstardom, Sidney always remains humble and gives back to his communities in Nova Scotia and Pennsylvania.

You can visit Sidney Crosby's actual dinged-up dryer at the Nova Scotia Sport Hall of Fame in Halifax, Nova Scotia.

Jai Agnish / Shutterstock.com